# THE ADVENTURES OF ARTHUR AND EDMUND

## A Tale of Two Seals

### BONTÉ DURAN

*A Margaret K. McElderry Book*

ATHENEUM     1984     NEW YORK

Library of Congress catalog card number: 83-071900

ISBN 0-689-50295-8

Printed in Great Britain

First American Edition

It was nap time at Seal Rocks. Arthur and Edmund did not like naps.
"Let's go for a swim," said Arthur. He and Edmund knew they were not
allowed to swim without their parents, but their parents were asleep.
"We could have a short swim," said Edmund.
"Follow me," said Arthur.

They slid down the wet seaweed into the water.

First they played hide-and-seek. Edmund hid.
"Why do you poke your nose out?" Arthur asked.
"I was afraid you wouldn't find me," said Edmund.

They had a diving contest.
"You are the best," said Arthur.
"Yes, I think I am," said Edmund.

Some fat fish swam by.
"I feel hungry," said Arthur.

"So do I," said a shark who poked his head out of a hole in the rock.
Arthur and Edmund did not like the way the shark smiled.
"Let's go home," said Edmund. They swam straight up to the surface of
the water and climbed out on the nearest rock.
The shark followed them.

"What's the hurry?" he asked. "Come back into the water and talk."
"We can talk here," said Arthur.
Edmund said, "I just saw some fish swim by. Why don't you chase them?"
"Good idea," said the shark. "But don't go away. I'll come straight back."

The shark swam off. "It was a polite shark," said Edmund.
"Let's get out of here," said Arthur.
They jumped into the water.

Deep under the water Arthur and Edmund swam and swam, hoping they were going in the opposite direction from the shark.
They felt very tired. "We'd better swim up and see where we are," said Arthur.

When they put their heads out of the water they saw a rocky island. The waves were very large and the little seals felt frightened.

"We'd better stay close together," said Edmund. "You can get lost behind a wave."

Then, by mistake, Edmund slid onto a nearby wave.
Arthur shouted, "Get back on *my* wave."
"I can't," called Edmund. "I'm on a new wave."

Edmund's wave turned him
over three times. He
landed between two rocks.

Arthur's wave brought
him in comfortably. He
saw Edmund was stuck.

"Are you hurt?" Arthur asked Edmund.
"I'm not hurt, I'm stuck," said Edmund. "Push me out."
Arthur pushed, but Edmund did not move.
Just then they saw a little girl. "There's a person," said Arthur.
"Perhaps the person will help me get unstuck," said Edmund.

The little girl's name was Lucy. She noticed Edmund stuck between the rocks and Arthur watching nervously.
"Can I help?" she called.

Lucy took hold of Edmund and gave a good tug. He came out more quickly than anyone expected. Arthur waited three rocks away. He had never been so close to a person, and felt worried.

"I have a picnic," Lucy said. "Would you like a peanut butter sandwich?"

"Is it a fish?" asked Edmund, and Arthur added, "Is it hard to catch?"

"You don't catch a peanut butter sandwich," Lucy said, "you make it."

The three friends sat down on the rocks. Lucy opened the picnic basket.
Arthur and Edmund did not like their peanut butter sandwich.
"Where is your cave?" Arthur asked Lucy.
"I don't live in a cave, I live in a house. Would you like to see it?"

The little seals were pleased to be invited to Lucy's house. They walked along the beach together and Edmund carried the picnic basket.

"There is my house," said Lucy.
"It's not at all like a cave," said Arthur. "It's too far from the water."
"It's very nice when you get inside," said Lucy.

Lucy helped Arthur and Edmund up the porch steps.
"Rocks are easier," said Edmund. "And there is no nice fishy smell here."
The three friends stood on the porch and looked across the water.
There were lots of small, rocky islands.
"I see our rocks," said Arthur, "we're not lost."
"That's a relief," said Edmund.

Inside the house Arthur and Edmund looked at everything.
"Where is the seaweed?" asked Edmund.
Arthur climbed into the fireplace. "This is like home," he said.

Lucy showed Arthur and Edmund how to rock in the rocking chairs.
"Have you noticed how rocking chairs make you sleepy?" asked Arthur.
"Yes," said Edmund. "I was just noticing . . ."
Both little seals went to sleep.

Meanwhile Lucy got the boat ready, and when Arthur and Edmund woke up she asked, "How would you like to go home in a boat?" The little seals were very excited. No one in their family had ever been in a boat before.

It was a long row back to Seal Rocks. Arthur looked over the side of the boat. Edmund trailed his flippers in the water and began to think how cross his mother would be. Arthur said, "Perhaps she will still be asleep."

The seals were all relaxing on the rocks, and at first they did not see the boat.

When they noticed it they slid into the water. Lucy could not row for fear of hitting someone's head.

Only the little seals' mother and father stayed on the rocks, looking cross and dignified.

"Arthur and Edmund, get out of that boat this moment," called their mother.

Both little seals jumped into the water. Edmund was better at swimming slowly than Arthur, so Arthur got there first. Their mother was so glad to see her children safe she only pretended to be cross.

"I must go home now," said Lucy. "We'll come and visit you," said the seals.
Lucy did not know how they would all fit into her porch, but she said, "Yes, you
must all come."

Arthur and Edmund felt tired. It had been a happy day.
They had not liked the shark, of course, or the peanut butter sandwiches,
or the big waves, but everything else had been perfect.
They fell asleep. . .

. . . and had a dream about their next visit to Lucy.
Lucy had the same dream.